With Love Always, Delilah

written by Micah C. Beachy

editing by L. Weary

I dedicate this book to anyone who has ever believed in me. Thank you for supporting my dreams. I love you all so much. And to everyone who hasn't believed in me, I don't dedicate this to you but I thank you for inspiring me to prove you wrong.

With love always,

M

Pleased To Meet Your Acquaintance

Hello, you. Yes, you...I don't quite know who you are which makes this an unknown territory. This is not a story, so if you're looking for a story, look further, because you won't find it here. This doesn't have a resolution either. No plot. No arch. It's just me talking to you, and telling you about my life so let's not make it complicated, okay? There are a few important things you should know about me before you continue to read this:

1. My name is Delilah, and names are very important, I think. How does one describe the artist, Leonardo da Vinci, without stating his name? Without names, you only have descriptions and though they might be accurate, they are only an opinion. Opinions are tricky little things for each person has a different outlook of the world than the next. If someone didn't know my name I could be described as that "blonde, wavy-haired girl with bad RBF and big boobs." I would rather just be called Delilah and not be reduced to my physical features, which happens frequently. I digress.

2. I fall in love easily. I like to look for the best in people, and when you only look for the good, it's easier to see love. That is one of my downfalls. There's a lot more to know about me, but we just got on a first name basis, so this is enough for now.

I am going to start by explaining the purpose of all of this to you, whoever you may be. I am going to be viciously honest with you through all of this. I tend to keep things bottled up, but carrying all of this around all the time and never sharing anything with anyone else is becoming increasingly more difficult. I am tired of holding back. I am tired of censoring myself. I am sick and tired of minding my manners so that people who don't give a damn about me can feel comfortable. I want this to be uncomfortable for you because it was for me. I also want you to find comfort and happiness in some of these accounts. From the movies I have watched, and the books that I have read, my sources confirm my theory that life is a happy blend of being terrified and ecstatic, and my life is no different.

I tend to be in my own head way too much. I can't stop thinking about if I am doing things the right way. Here lies the issue: Betty. I feel as if I have all of this stuff inside of me, boiling up and eating me away. It's as if, within my subconscious, there is an evil witch residing in a gingerbread house luring in the most vulnerable parts of me. I have decided that the witch's name is Betty. She was a problem when I was weak and developing; we are kind of friends now. I say kind of because she does not come around as often as she used to.

Speaking of friends, though they would never admit to it, I can tell that my best friends are all tired of hearing my problems. I am tired of hearing my problems too, but I can feel my friends slowing slipping into boredom when I start talking about things that really bother me. And you might say "well, get new friends," but my friends are incredible - they just have a lot of their own burdens to carry, so they really don't need mine weighing them down, too.

And this isn't the kind of stuff I would want to talk to my parents about. My dad would feel awkward, and my mom wants me focused on the "bigger picture," which means I have been keeping my thoughts to myself… but that isn't really working either. I have thought of keeping a diary, but it feels like an irrelevant solution to a large problem. It is true - I want to write; I just want to write without parameters. If I took up journaling, I would feel like I had a daily obligation. In a diary, I can't backspace, I can't reword sentences to better get my point across to you, and I need you to get this. I mean really get this. I am not wasting my own time, or yours, clear?

I'm sad and I'm really happy too, all at once. I guess most people are like that. I've heard that, at least, that people get sad for no reason, but people always seem to have a reason to be happy. I have a real reason though. A few. For both categories. I feel very mixed up about all of this so I won't cry to you on day one. I will ease you into it. I'm not great with first impressions. I am awkward. This feels awkward. Here we go. Okay.

Let me try this again! Hi, nice to meet you. My name is Delilah. Buckle up, or something like that.

With love always,

Delilah

P.S. Music and art, artistry – that sort of thing…
it's all a big part of who I am. I decided to insert
some playlists for you so that you can understand
what kind of state I was in for some of these
accounts. If you're the kind of person that likes to
read the last page of a book before you finish it,
listen to the playlists before you read my chapter.
If you're the type of person who doesn't read the
last page of the book until you finish it,
chronological order works swell, too. Let's get
started.

<u>Delilah's Playlist #1</u>

Robbers - The 1975

I Wanna Get Better - Bleachers

Video Games - Lana Del Rey

Ship to Wreck - Florence and the Machine

Slow It Down - The Lumineers

Cherry Wine - Hozier

You Don't Know Me (feat. Regina Spektor) - Ben Folds

My First Friend

Blonde, beautiful, young, kind –

I was her best friend, she was mine.

Catching the bus on the first day of school

both of us carrying princess lunchboxes, in style and

so cool.

Conquering 18 years of battles together –

Enduring storms that other relationships did not

weather.

Still as there for her, as she is for me,

I am lucky to have such an incredible life-long
friend

–

B.E.B.

MOO!

(Alternative Header: The Demise of My Self-Confidence)

Hello you no-name slob,

I am taking a leap of faith. I'm about to open up to you, it's really hard for me to do that with anyone, but don't you worry; I'll get there, and I'll get you there… I just need to set up everything for you. I need to make you understand, do you know what I mean? Maybe not right now, but you will.

I have never been the most confident person. Well, actually, come to think of it I was pretty confident up until eighth grade. You see in eighth grade, I had some extra weight (read as: it was a baby fat and puberty cocktail). Woof. Plus, I had C-cup boobs. Big C-cup boobs. Boys my age were not exactly good at talking to me, as their attention was always drawn to my big C-cup boobs. "Yes, they're real," "no I don't stuff," and "no, I won't show you to prove that I don't stuff" were a few of my normal catchphrases wandering the halls of that horrid middle school.

Going into my eighth-grade year, I decided to be bolder, to flourish as a social butterfly so I decided to go to the popular guy's birthday party. It was still when boys and girls did not exactly mingle well. The boys were all gathered around the stereo system and the girls were talking by an idle television. I was sitting in a recliner, with my back to the guys, chatting with a few acquaintances. None of my close friends were at the party - Andy and Kait (two of my best friends who will be mentioned later) didn't attend that sort of thing, so I was the odd man out. I tried to be social with everyone though, and it was pleasant enough. I was doing my best to feel (or at least appear to feel) comfortable when I was flipped out of the recliner by two boys, Jaden and Mitchell. They followed the act with a phrase that in the following days would become popular amongst my peers: "that's what we call cow tipping!"

I will never forget those little greasy assholes (who turned into big greasy assholes). Thinking about it now, when I close my eyes, I can still see them hovering over me, warped looks on their faces, and I feel the fear re-enter my body. I feel like hiding again, like before.

Despite their greasy asshole-ness, everyone laughed hysterically at their prank (everyone except for me, of course). I went home that night super sad, but I wanted people to like me, I wanted to have friends, so I put my personal issues on the back burner.

When I went got ready for school the following Monday morning, I took a little extra time on myself. I wore a denim jacket over a fitted Hollister shirt (because Hollister shirts were the hot thing then) and a long and flattering skirt. Walking into school and down the hall to my locker, I felt pretty, until...

I heard...

Them mooing at me.

Yes. Mooing (i.e., cow noises). At first, I thought someone was just making noises, but then I remembered the recliner incident from the birthday party. As I walked by the lockers, and my classmates, that dreadful noise occurred on a sound loop. I had no idea how the trend caught on; it's as if they had some sort of secret organization that met on Sunday evenings to discuss how to destroy someone, and this week their target was me.

A day passed, a week passed, a month passed, and they didn't tire of it. I would try to push it away, but I was mortified. Any value I had was gone. I buried myself in school and basketball. Basketball was a good way for me to relieve some of the aggression that was building up inside of me. Basketball kept my mind off of those evil little boys. Better yet, basketball kept me in shape.

The month was March, March of 2011. Our school was doing a fundraiser: the students paid a dollar to watch a student vs. teachers basketball game during school hours. I was good at basketball, so good that I was a starter on the eighth-grade girl's middle school team. When it came time for the girls to come in the game, I took my position (ya know, postin' up). A teammate passed the ball to me, and as I was going up to shoot, I heard the entire eighth-grade section mooing... at me... in front of the entire school, and no one did anything about it. I wanted the floor to cave in. I wanted to run. To go hide somewhere. To cry. I wanted my mom. I wanted to be anywhere but right there. Instead, time started to slow down. I tuned out the incident for a moment, turned inwards, and said to myself "I can't let them know that they have that much of an effect on me".

The rest of the day felt like it was happening in slow motion. Instead of walking through normal air, the texture I moved through felt heavy, and sticky, and uncomfortable - molasses. With every step I took, I felt a ripple shake the extra skin on my body. One step. Stomach. Another. A thigh. Another. My face.

That night I went home and cried until my eyes felt like they were bleeding. Tired and out of tears, I stood in front of the mirror. I remember I used to see a girl in that reflection who I was proud of. Where did I go wrong? When did she go missing? How can I find her again? How can I get rid of this blubber monster that crowds my reflection?

In reality, I was a hundred and forty pounds, wearing a size eight jeans… but in the mirror that night I was two hundred thousand pounds and wearing a size 1 million jeans.

I hated what I saw, so I decided to change it. I started waking up at 5 AM to work out in the basement (so I wouldn't wake my parents). Before basketball practice, I ran suicide sprints in the road. Before bed, I did 200 sit ups and 300 squats. No matter how hard I worked out, the image in the mirror never budged.

Desperate for my body to change, I looked for short-cuts. I thought back to a time when I was sick and throwing up a few times an hour. I remembered how thin I looked after being sick. In hopes of similar results, I started eating large meals… every meal was a feast. At my feasts, I had brownies, cookies, pizza, bread, anything I wanted. Then, moments after the feast, I tossed it all back into the toilet. Doing so made me feel better. I felt thinner and in control of my situation. I had the power to have my cake and eat it too and get rid of it so it didn't go straight to my thighs or my belly or my hips.

Naturally, one of my friends, Andy, found out and told a teacher who then called me into her office. She told me that she knew what I had been doing. I told her why. She held me while I cried. It was the first time that I had ever mentioned the situation to anyone out loud. I had been keeping everything built up inside. Telling her, saying the words to someone who seemed like they really cared about me, was the first step I needed to get better. The teacher asked me how long I had been doing it, and I told her only two weeks. She told me that if I kept on this path that my teeth would turn nasty and my hair would fall out. Then, she confided to me that she had been struggling with anorexia her whole life. It was so bad that she had to go to a rehabilitation center for it. She asked me if I needed that kind of help, and I told her I didn't. The idea of having to leave my family or go away to a center scared me and it seemed like more of a punishment than a solution. It turns out, I just needed someone in that school to really understand what I was going through and to care about me, and she did. That same week, I stopped altogether. She had me keep a food and exercise journal so that I could track my habits. When someone would do something mean or make me feel bad, I went to her and we would jump rope together. I started feeling safe at school again. She made me excited to come to school. During some of our conversations, she would ask me who was doing the stuff to me that made me feel bad. I didn't want to get anyone in trouble, and despite everything, I still craved their friendship. She understood that. She was a safety net for me and no one knew. I'm not sure that she even told other members of the administration. Naturally, she and I developed a close bond, and on the last day of school, while others were excited to be moving to high school, I became scared to leave my safety net. I was worried about what my life would be like without her. I was becoming stronger every day but I absolutely did not feel ready to be on my own. Instead of dismissing my fears and sending me off to class, together we developed a food and exercise plan for my summer. I wanted to continue to be a cheerleader in high school, and she advised that cheerleading would be a good thing for me. She said that the girls look out for each other and it would keep me in shape. I hugged her tightly one last time and thanked her for everything she had done for me.

The summer after eighth grade, I lost fifteen more pounds, my braces came off, I dyed my hair blonde, and I started feeling beautiful again. That was probably one of the happiest times of my life.

As the warm days of summer started to dwindle, an icy fear crept back in. The day before my first year of high school started, I cried again. Despite how beautiful I had been feeling, I was so worried that the old habits of my peers (and of myself) would find their way to me in high school.

On the first day of school, two blocks went by, and I thanked my lucky stars that no one was no mooing.

I was so totally, utterly (ha), relieved.

I thought that since I was a cheerleader now that everyone would like me and respect me. I was wrong. At lunch, when the inevitable sounds came again, I felt like I was moving backward. I went to the bathroom and cried my eyes out, thinking over and over: "why can't you be stronger than this?!". My thoughts were interrupted by someone calling out my name, "Delilah?" she paused, "I saw you come in here. Are you okay?" It was Laurel, one of the senior cheerleaders who was always nice to me, even when I almost dropped our flyer during stunt groups on her head. I came out of the stall and collapsed into her which made me cry harder. She held me and calmed me down so that I could tell her what had been happening for the past six months (making her the second person I had ever confided in).

Laurel told the football coach who then seriously reprimanded the boys on the team. My boyfriend and his friends who were seniors football players had some barring over the underclassmen who were being so cruel to me. They mentioned kicking some freshmen butt during football practice if the guys continued to be nasty towards me. It felt like things were going to be okay, but I was never the same after all of that. I did not want to be some damsel in distress, but people were protecting me, and it felt good to have people on my side, but I wanted to just be normal and to not need rescuing at all.

That night at football practice, the boys who were mean to me all had to run hills from start to finish. They had a stern talking to and poof, it went away.

To this day, I still get a weird feeling in my belly when I hear someone make a mooing sound. A child, a teen, an adult — it doesn't matter who. I wish my self-confidence would have reappeared so easily. It was gone for a long time after that. Those mean, razor-tongued boys basically built Betty's gingerbread house for her. They planted that wicked witch inside of my head that hadn't previously been there. I wish I had been as strong as Gretel to push the witch into the oven, but I was weak. I felt like a plump Hansel, trapped in a cage… except the cage was my own mind and the witch didn't have the key to it. I did. And I still couldn't escape it.

With love always,

Delilah

<u>Delilah's Playlist #2</u>

Outside Looking In – Jordan Pruitt

Mean – Taylor Swift

Perfect – P!nk

What Now - Rihanna

Breakaway – Kelly Clarkson

Mind Your Manners – Chiddy Bang

Suddenly I See – KT Tunstall

The Gingerbread House's Chapter

Hello Confidant,

At this point, you might've heard me mention a witch living inside of a gingerbread house that is inside of my head. She has been with me the majority of my adolescent life into young adulthood and because of that, I thought Betty deserved some recognition. Yes, my little monster's name is Betty. Betty changes colors, sometimes she is red, blue, pink, or any other color of the rainbow that she feels like being. She identifies as a female. Betty can be a real bitch sometimes. On a day that I feel really dressed up and pretty, she will pop in her evil little voice in my head and tell me "you look like a fat cow in that!" Sometimes, though, she will tell me that I am a rock star.

We had a very abusive relationship when I younger; she was really mean to me. When I was a freshman in high school, she would tell me things like "no one wants you around", "no one really loves you", "you're a bother to everyone in your life", and it was hard to tune her out. Remember those mean boys? Yeah, well they created her. They basically stuffed the recipe in my ear to construct her; she was a product of cruelty.

When she would make me cry, to drown out her harsh words I turned on music from my favorite bands like The Lumineers, or I watched Audrey Hepburn movies, dreamed of the day I would get out the country, and thought of a life living in NYC or Paris or London that would make me proud some day.

After a while, I had enough of stupid, evil Betty. I decided I would not let a bitch like her ruin my life. I started doing yoga, I put more effort into acting which was my passion (I read and watched a lot theatre), I spent more time writing, I laughed more, I tried to go on more adventures, to smile more, to spend a lot of time with people who loved me. Because I started loving my life, despite Betty's mean comments, she grew to respect me. Those evil words started becoming more and more scarce.

It's taken seven years but Betty and I have a pretty healthy relationship now. It helped that I upgraded her gingerbread rancher into a penthouse suite.

Sometimes she rears her ugly head around PMS time for the occasional "your face looks like the moon today" but for the most part, she tells me that I'm a really cool person and she reminds me of all the things that I've done to get where I am now. I guess we'll always have an estranged relationship until the very end. I am okay with that now though because every day I am becoming more comfortable with the person that I am. It is unlikely that I am always going to be glowing with self-confidence; I admire anyone who is but that's just not me.

I am happy that I have been able to overcome and live peacefully with Betty. If you have your own Betty, or whomever, I hope you can get to this point that I am at. I recommend finding out what your passion is and throwing yourself at it every day. Never lose sight of your dreams.

With love always,

Delilah (and Betty)

<u>Blocking Out Betty Playlist</u>

Love Myself – Hailee Steinfeld

These Words – Natasha Bedingfield

My Beloved Monster – The Eels

Dog Days Are Over – Florence and the Machine

Shake it Out – Florence and the Machine

You Will Be Found – Dear Evan Hansen

Rivers and Roads – The Head and the Heart

Don't You Cry For Me (Acoustic) – Cobi

Glorious – Macklemore

Tequila Moonrise

You stayed. You haven't stopped or given up on me, yet... that's surprising.

I don't know that I can call you friend quite so soon but we're building something here, can you feel it? ... so let's stick with this, "confidant".

Hello Confidant,

I hope you're doing well today. I am. I just got finished grocery shopping. Actually, it's kind of funny. Now when I go grocery shopping, I go into the liquor section just because I can. Rarely do I buy anything, but being twenty-one years old it's nice to finally be able to have the freedom to enter the forbidden zones. While in that VIP section one afternoon I saw a bottle of tequila, and instantly I was a curious fourteen-year-old girl again. You see, when I was fourteen I had my first shot of tequila. It was nearly midnight and I was with two of my life-long friends, Andy and Kait. Andy, Kait, and I have been friends since we were all five years old. We were even in the same kindergarten class. Kait moved around some growing up but she always found her way back to Andy and me.

One night, we were bored at Andy's house and we all decided we wanted to try something new. Instead of learning how to French braid or watching planking tutorials on YouTube, we broke into Andy's parents' liquor cabinet for a wild time. Andy grabbed salt, because she had heard her mom talking about "chasers." We had one shot, then another, and another. By the third, I started to get tingly, but not "drunk," I didn't really want to be "drunk." But Andy and Kait… they got hammered. We laughed a lot. We talked about any number of things that popped into our intoxicated minds, ever so often throwing in the occasional, "wow my hands feel weird" comment. Soon, we got bored again. We wanted to do something else that none of us had done before - we wanted to streak.

Within no time we had all agreed to take our clothes off and go streaking down Andy's gravel driveway. It was so dark outside, but a full moon lit the sky just enough for us. We all walked out holding each other's hands. Together we giggled and counted 1…2…3… and just like that we began quickly undressing. I tore off my shirt, (it felt exhilarating), kicked my Old Navy flip flops off into the darkness, and pulled down my shorts. As my shorts dropped down around my ankles, I hesitated... I started thinking of everything that could be dangerous about what I was doing. The second my hesitation kicked in, in my peripherals I saw my best friends continuing to rapidly disrobe and their courage made my mind go on autopilot. I took a deep breath in, and then I ran for my life. I remember feeling the sharp, cold pieces of gravel underneath my feet - they hurt but I laughed, I laughed so hard. I felt free. I looked to either side of me and there were my friends, laughing and tipsy; nearly tripping over their own feet. I half hoped my friend's neighbor, a high school boy, had seen us do it. But I think only the stars saw us that night, and that was probably best for us.

With love always,

Delilah

Free Bird - Lynard Skynrd

Marie's Chapter

(Alternative Header: The girl who taught me how to properly name my inanimate objects)

Hello Confidant,

For all the pain that I have endured, I have experienced 1000x more happiness. One of the people who has brought some of the happiest times into my life is a girl named Marie. Marie was my best friend growing up. We're still close now, but back then we were inseparable. If you saw me, Marie was usually close by and vice versa. She helped me become the person I am today, truly. She taught me how to be bold, how to see the beauty in things, and how to believe in myself. In the times when I most needed it, she was always there to hug me and tell me "everything will be okay." When I doubted myself, she would say things like "THE 21ST CENTURY IS A PLACE WHERE HOMELESS BOYS ARE VALEDICTORIANS AND FIRST-GENERATION IMMIGRANTS GRADUATE FROM COLLEGE WITH HONORS AND PEOPLE GET FAMOUS FOR BEING A TARGET BAG BOY AND 10 YEAR OLDS START CHARITIES AND DOGS CAN BE PHOTOGRAPHERS SO WHY CAN'T YOU BE WHAT YOU WANT? WHO MADE MY CINNAMON BUN FEEL SO PESSIMITIC? WHO STOLE

YOUR CINNAMON?" (an actual quote from our sophomore year of high school)

One time a boy broke my heart and she brought over a remedy of Kleenex, stuffed crust cheese pizza from Pizza Hut, Pringles Cheezums, Ben and Jerry's Half-Baked ice cream, Trolli Sour Brite Crawlers, Little Debbie Swiss Rolls, Starbucks, and a Brisk pink lemonade – all of my very favorite snack foods. That boy (who you will hear about in a later chapter) broke my heart at 8 PM, and Marie was at my house by 9 PM with the aforementioned comforts and an ear ready to listen. That was one of the best things about her - she always listened, and she never tried to give advice unless it was asked for. When it (advice) was requested, she gave the best kind. It attacked the issue and provided a practical solution. When I got back with the boy who broke my heart (stupidly), she did not judge me. When he broke up with me two days before my 18th birthday, she made sure to bring my birthday present to school the next day so that I would have something to smile about.

Usually, I got to school before Marie, but that morning she must have left her house early to beat me to the auditorium where we had our first class. I didn't really want to go to school that morning because my heart was hurting. I walked down the runway of the auditorium and she was sitting in her seat (which was next to mine) and she said: "close your eyes." Without hesitation, I listened, and I felt a something plop into my hands. I opened my eyes and saw a beautiful robin's-egg colored blue box tied up with a white ribbon. My eyes filled with water and a smile swept over my face. I hadn't even seen the contents of the box, but I was already so happy, not just because of the present, but because of the thoughtfulness and the love. I was, and continue to be, a lover of *Breakfast at Tiffany's*. It is my favorite movie and Audrey Hepburn is my favorite actress. Though I was smitten over *B@T*, I was just 18 years old and had never been in the right financial position to purchase anything from the iconic brand. I guess Marie decided I should have something. The bracelet was delicate and beautiful, like her, like us.

She was the kind of friend who became more like a sister. As far as my parents were concerned, she was their second daughter. If there was a family event, Marie was always invited.

In the summer, we would stay up all night listening to music, watching new shows, and online shopping for our future prom dresses. When we got bored, we would make music videos. We always knew how to entertain ourselves. We fought a few times, too — most sisters do. I don't want to tell you about the bad in our relationship. We fought sometimes, all friends do, with Marie and I, the good outweighs any of the bad. I have a few favorite memories with Marie. And here are my favorite ones, in no particular order:

1. *The first time sneaking out*
2. *Dominos pizza and scary movies*
3. *Moving around my bedroom in the late hours of the night*
4. *Performing*

And hopefully, you want to know the words behind the list? Well, regardless I'm going to tell you…

The first time I ever snuck out was out of Marie's bedroom window. We were talking about all of the naughty things we had done, and when she mentioned sneaking out… well, that was one of the things I had never experienced and I told her that. Within seconds she was hurrying me to grab my shoes.

She turned up the music on her speaker, locked her bedroom door, and we began making our way out. She climbed through the window and landed quietly on her front yard. She told me to be quiet because her mother's window was right beneath hers. I hesitantly straddled the window, and with a deep breath, I threw my leg around and landed not so silently in the yard – officially a rebel. Once we were out, we didn't go to any place in particular. We walked around her neighborhood, swung on the swings at the playground, but that was the extent of it. After about thirty minutes of the criminal lifestyle, we climbed back into her bedroom, turned down the stereo, and got ready for bed. It might not seem like a lot to you, but to me it was everything.

Marie pushed me. She always got me to try new things. After ordering perhaps our hundredth pizza, she made me sit on the couch and watch a scary alien movie… I hated it, but she insisted it was something new that I should try. I love my comfort zone, but I was happy to have someone to frequently pull me out of it. She was always so ready to tackle anything I threw at her, too. One summer night, I called her around 11 P.M., and I told her I needed a change. Thirty minutes later, she was backed into a wall helping me shift my bed frame and rearrange my entire bedroom. Another time, she dressed up as Santa – fat suit and everything – to be my partner in a comedy skit at school. Everyone laughed (in a good way). She was also beautifully talented in singing – her voice sounded like an angel's, it was light and airy but strong when need be (like her).

She is away now, in Wisconsin studying Psychology, and every day I miss her. We might be two completely different people now than we were back then, but she made my experience in high school (the good parts) what it was. I continue to miss her, and root for her, every single day. I doubt I will ever stop. I hope every single one of her dreams come true.

With love always,

Delilah

Marie's Playlist

Tongue Tied - Grouplove

Aberdeen - Cage the Elephant

It's Time - Imagine Dragons

I Like It Like That - Hot Chelle Ray

Call Me Maybe - Carly Rae Jepsen

Thrift Shop - Macklemore

Schoolboy - Grouplove

The Middle - Jimmy Eat World

She Will Be Loved - Maroon 5

Nine in the Afternoon - Panic! At the Disco

This Is What Makes Us Girls - Lana Del Rey

Charles's Chapter

Hello Confidant,

Today, I feel like traveling back in time and telling you the story of the first guy who ever really let me down. I liked him, a lot. I say like because it wasn't love, I was infatuated with him, but it was as close to love as I had been at fourteen.

I was an eighth grader going on a tour of the almighty high school that I would be attending after summer break. My tour guides were two junior guys who were about to be seniors on the varsity football team. They were both cute, and I was intrigued by both of them, but something about the one on the right with the bright blue eyes and dark brown, almost black hair caught my attention. I was about to be a freshman cheerleader and I adored the idea of dating a senior football player. It helped that I thought he was quite a cutie, too.

I told my girlfriend Andy that the tour guide with the dark brown hair, Charles, was going to be my boyfriend. "Mark my words," I said to her, "we will be together." I was absolutely smitten but I was also very shy. Instead of approaching him, I did what any fourteen-year-old girl would do: I stalked him on Facebook (I could've told you the name of his second cousin and what color dress shirt he wore to his freshman homecoming dance). After scrolling his page for a few hours, I gathered up my courage and sent him a message on Facebook:

"Thanks for the great tour today!"

He replied, "Anytime, if you ever need help my locker is the one right between the water fountain and the library."

Even as I write this, I can remember how warm my body felt and how quickly my heart pulsed. That conversation led to another, which led to some flirting, which led to my chance.

His best friend Aaron and my friend Elaine started casually dating. Then, Aaron invited Elaine, Charles, and I over to his house to go swimming at the lake. My dad was hesitant about me hanging out with a senior boy, but my mom could tell how much I liked him and convinced him to let me go. In the car ride over, I went through a checklist in my head: "did I shave all of the hair off of my armpits? Goodness, I hope so. I certainly don't want Charles to know that I grow hair. Did I pack a pair of underwear for after we swim? Yes, okay, I did. Deodorant? Check."

When I got to the lake, Aaron, Elaine, and Charles were already in the water, putting the spotlight on me (something I would normally enjoy, but not half-naked at fourteen. Please remember at this time, I was just starting to gain back the self-confidence I had lost in the previous months). As I waded into the water, Elaine swam over to me and told me that Charles had been bugging her about what time I would be there. It made me really happy to hear that. Elaine and I gabbed about different sorts of things for a moment: cheerleading, music, until Charles and Aaron swam over to us. Charles asked me how I was, to which I shyly answered, "I'm well."

"Stop being so shy," he responded, and I splashed him for that. He splashed me back. Soon, Elaine and Aaron broke away from us and I was swimming in my own little world with Charles.

We talked and talked but I can't remember now what about. All I remember is how good his muscles looked while the water rippled around, and how blue his eyes were. They really sparkled from the sun and water. After another splash fight and lots of smiling and laughing, he pulled me in. My legs fell over his and we laughed and smiled together. No kissing, no moves, just blissful happiness, and that's how we spent the next twenty minutes.

When the sky began to darken, threatening rain, the four of us went back to Aaron's house and "watched a movie" in his rec room (spoiler: none of us actually watched the movie). Elaine and Aaron sat on the couch together, and Charles and I laid down on the floor. Against the floor, I could feel that I had a sunburn, making me thrice more warm but also cold. I wanted to snuggle up to Charles, but I didn't want to cross any lines. With him next to me, my inside started to heat up, too. Within moments of the movie starting, Aaron and Elaine pulled the blanket over them for some privacy. I wondered what Charles and I would do with our newly gained privacy. I really liked him and I wanted him to like me too, and respect me. Though he wouldn't have been my first kiss, I wanted *our* first kiss to be special.

My thoughts were interrupted by him asking if I
wanted to step outside for a second. We sat on the
porch and listened to the rain. Sitting on his lap,
my head resting on his shoulder, he gently kissed
first my forehead, and then my lips. The world
stopped. All of the noise – the sound of the rain,
the trees, the birds – everything fell silent. When I
opened my eyes, he was smiling back at me. It was
almost as if he had read my mind about wanting a
special first kiss between us. Him kissing me made
something inside of me start to tingle. We kissed
again, and again, and then we went back to our floor
spot in the rec room and made out. It was the first
time I had really ever made out with someone but he
was hot, and kissing him was hot. I felt good. After
our date, I thought to myself, "I got him."

The annual county fair was only two weeks away
and I was excited by the idea that Charles and I
could ride the Ferris Wheel and hopefully get stuck
at the top together. But Charles never mentioned
going with me. After our lake adventure, I texted him
here and there, but he hardly ever responded. I knew
he was busy with football conditioning and I was busy
with cheerleading, too, so I didn't think much of it.

At the fair's opening night, I ran into Aaron, who instead of calling me Delilah, called me "that girl who made out with Charles." I didn't like that. A few minutes later, I saw Charles… holding hands with another girl… yikes… *definitely* didn't like that. Her name was Mille and they had been an on-and-off thing, and I guess sometime between the lake and the fair, they turned back on... making him and I an *off* thing.

I didn't like how abruptly things had dropped off between Charles and me, but I felt surprisingly and pleasantly resilient. When the school year started, I went on dates with other guys, and eventually started seeing a boy named Peter pretty regularly. He was also on the football team, so after the games I would give him a peck on the cheek or a hug, mostly because I wanted to, but also because I got some pleasure out of knowing that Charles could see us (I had heard some rumors that he was jealous of Peter and I but wasn't sure how true they were). I got my answer in late November when Charles texted me to ask if I would join him on a school trip to D.C. Though I hesitated to say yes, given his previous behavior, a part of me still liked him a lot, so I stopped seeing

Peter and I agreed to go on the D.C. trip with
Charles.

In D.C. we felt like a couple, though we had
never clarified what we were. I didn't ask because I
was scared of ruining the moment and of hearing his
answer. The best part of being in D.C. with him,
though, was when we went over to the Christmas trees.
We stood in front of them, and looking at the
twinkling lights, he held my hand. I was reluctant to
hold back, but then he pulled me closer (like he had
the summer before in the lake). I started to feel all
warm and fuzzy again. I remember feeling like I
wanted him to kiss me, but he didn't and that didn't
disappoint me for some reason. Something inside of me
told me to just be patient. Hours later, back at the
high school, he walked me to his truck and opened the
door for me (he always opened the door for me - I
loved that a lot). It was very cold out, so cold that
there was frost on the windshield. He had an older
truck so it took a while to heat up. We sat for a
moment, and Charles must have noticed the goosebumps
on my arms because offered me his varsity jacket. I
wore it proudly for the entirety of the twenty-minute
drive, all the while holding his hand tightly while
he navigated the windy roads back to my house. In my

driveway, the Christmas lights on my house made us glow. He walked me to the front door where I thanked him for the ride home and started to take off his jacket. He told me to keep it and hugged me tightly. Our bodies felt so warm pressed up against each other in the cold climate. He was taller than me, so his chin rested perfectly on my head. I felt my heart start picking up. It was beating faster and faster. I got self-conscious. I wondered if he could hear it pounding, too. Without loosening his grip around me, he asked if I would be his girlfriend. I nodded yes and looked up for his reaction. When our eyes met, he leaned into me, slipped his hand around the base of my neck, and kissed me so sweetly that my knees felt weak. It felt just like the first time, but better. We became inseparable.

In between classes at school, Charles would find me at the end of one to walk me to the beginning of another. We held hands while walking, and if my books were heavy, he would carry them for me. I felt so honored to be holding his hand in front of the entire school. After practices, he offered to give me a ride home. Some mornings he picked up for school and would bring me coffee. We spent weekends together, too. Sometimes, we would go out to dinner, or to the cinema but usually, we just hung out in his downstairs living room "watching movies". We kissed a lot. With every kiss we shared, a sexual tension became increasingly obvious between us.

Occasionally he would mention being worried that I was too young for him, but I always told him I was mature for my age and that it balanced out since guys mature two years slower than girls. That made him laugh. One of my favorite memories of us together was Christmas Eve. He came over around noon to exchange presents. After the gift swap, we walked through my neighborhood, and then retired to my room. While we were in my bedroom, he mentioned me going to his family's church service with him. I'm not religious, but I wanted to be with him as long as possible, so I went to church. It confused me. There was a lot of singing and that part was nice. They were Christmas songs, so I knew them well enough to sing along.

After the church service, we went back to his house with his family and had pizza, and then he drove me home. My mom saw us pulling up. She greeted us on the porch and told Charles to come in and grab some Christmas cookies. While we were dunking my mother's delicious chocolate chip cookies in cold milk, my parents went upstairs to wrap my brother and I's presents. While sitting at the table, Charles began humming "Have Yourself a Merry Little Christmas", which then turned into him singing into his milk glass. Within moments, to my pleasant surprise, he swept me up off of my feet and started dancing with me in my kitchen.

T'was the night before Christmas and I was so happy. I had no way of knowing, the next month together would be crappy.

Those were some of the happiest moments I had with Charles. Our relationship lasted into January. He drove me to the basketball games that I cheered at. He always sat in the crowd and made faces at me while I cheered. Walking in, he carried my heavy cheer bag and always let me wear his varsity jacket. Like I said, I felt really happy. Where did things go wrong? Well, Charles and I were intimate but never fully intimate… if you know what I mean. We didn't ever have sex. I wasn't sure I was ready, and he didn't think I was ready. In the moments when I felt ready, he said no, that he wasn't comfortable. In the moments when he felt ready, I said no, I wasn't comfortable. So it never happened, and because of that, this did:

On Monday morning, January 12th, my good friend Brad, who wrestled with Charles, wouldn't make eye contact with me. It was strange. Almost as strange as Charles ignoring me all day Sunday. I had a weird feeling in the pit of my stomach but I pushed it away and diagnosed myself with the Monday blues. At lunch, Brad, Marie, and Scarlett and I all sat at the table, and typically, we couldn't stop talking to one another but things were eerily quiet. After a few uncomfortable moments, I asked Brad why he had been avoiding me and he told me that he had something to tell me that he didn't want to tell me: Charles had cheated on me. Not only did Charles cheat on me, but he cheated on me with Millie. Not only did Charles cheat on me with Millie, but he walked into wrestling practice bragging about it and Brad had overheard. I asked Charles about it; he told the truth and we broke up. I cried a little. A lot. I liked what he and I had. I liked how he made me feel and I was sad it was over.

After that, I passed him in the hallways. It always seemed like he was still looking out for me, despite the fact he betrayed me. He graduated, and he went into the Navy. He dated Millie for awhile then but something happened: Charles got discharged for a bad hip and when he got back that August, he found out Millie had been seeing someone else behind his back. Charles came to me for comfort and I was there for him.

One night, we were at a common friend's pool party, and he started talking to me again. He was very flirtatious and charming, just like before. He offered to give me a ride home and I fell into it. I walked over to his truck, and I thought he was coming around the side of the truck to open the door for me like before, but then he pushed me up against his truck, slipped his hands around my waist and kissed me hard… it felt good for a split second. As he was kissing me… I felt an uneasy feeling. It was the realization that I was the second choice. A plan b. A second resort for him…when he had been my first choice every day of the week for the previous year and a half. I stopped kissing him, thanked him for the offer but decided to go back to the party and wait for my mom to pick me up. After that, it was really over. I saw him sometimes at football games while I was cheering. He would be with his friends,

they would be in an alumni section together cheering
for the team, but I didn't ever feel that warm
feeling. It was always cold when I looked at him. And
it hurt.

It was weird when it was over. Some of the
breakups I have had since Charles have felt like they
have business left to them, but our relationship
never did. I don't know if it was the cheating, or
that ultimately I knew our lives were going in two
very different directions. Despite everything, I
vividly remember the good parts of our relationship
and I am thankful for those feelings and experiences
I had. I wish him well too. He is getting married
next month. That's one thing I have a hard time with
when it comes to exes. I don't want them, but the
thought that I wasn't the one for someone is a little
painful, but then I feel guilty for being selfish and
it's a big mess. I try to resolve my internal
conflict by reminding myself that when I meet my "the
one", none of it will matter. And if Charles were
right in front of me, right now, I would smile at
him, probably get nervous and start to feel like that
fourteen-year-old girl again, but I would be happy we
both ended up where we are. I hope his marriage is

his happily ever after. I hope someday mine will be, too.

With love always,

Delilah

<u>Charles's Playlist</u>

Dirt Road Anthem — Jason Aldean

The Boys of Fall — Kenny Chesney

Just A Kiss — Lady Antebellum

A Lonely September — Plain White T's

Enchanted — Taylor Swift

Mistletoe — Justin Bieber

I do not like country music but I did for that brief relationship.

Go! Fight! Interlude

Hello Confidant,

There are some things in life that I will never
forget.

The drum cadences and motions to:

"eat 'em up, eat 'em up, go big blue"

are two of those things.

With love always,

Delilah

Power Interlude

Hello Confidant,

I once had a crush on a guy who taught me how to use power tools.

—

Though we did have chemistry, we never dated. He seemed to respect me enough, though, despite the fact that I was less experienced than him.

—

Maybe the secret to a respectful relationship is establishing that both parties are able to operate heavy, dangerous machinery, and then putting trust in their ability to do so.

With love always,

Delilah

McKenzie's Chapter

Hello Confidant,

I hope you're doing well today. I am, if you are wondering. This is a story about a girl that I miss. A lot. Our friendship started in the 6th grade, with me shoving her off of her chair so that I could talk to another person in a group project. I didn't meaannn to shove her off, but her poor little butt fell right on the ground. Then I realized how rude I was, apologized, and introduced myself. We were instant friends. Middle school was better with McKenzie. At one point, our middle school did a production of Seussical the Musical. McKenzie was Mayzie La Bird and I was the Sour Kangaroo. There was so much sass happening in the production and it was wonderful to have my best friend by my side for all of it.

Theatre together was fun but the peak of our friendship was the summer before high school when McKenzie and I were both trying out for the cheerleading squad together. We were dedicated. Every day before practice, she and I would take webcam videos of our routines to make sure we were doing them perfectly. We practiced in the pool, by the pool, in the grass, on the concrete – anywhere we could. That summer Kenz and I had all sorts of adventures in tandem with cheerleading tryouts. Our adventures were so legit I had a whole Facebook album dedicated to the "Stupid Adventures of Delilah and Kenz." It was when planking was still a popular thing, so we obviously did a lot of that. Oooo and it was when taking webcam pictures was all the rage so there were a million webcam pictures of us with things like a watermelon head or a shark face. Just your standard 14-year-old girl, 2011 behavior. A week before the tryouts, Kenz and I had a camping night at my grandparent's pool. We made s'mores, talked about boys, talked to boys – my grandparent's neighbor was a boy named Brett who was in our class and about to be a football player, so we walked over and chatted with him a bit to see how practices and things were going. Kenz was dating a guy named Cal at the time and we both thought it was lurvvvvv. Again 14. What I'm saying is, we had fun. We had so much fun.

On the day the squad was announced, I remember running up to the door with her, holding her hand. We both spotted our names and hugged each other and squealed. Then we let go of each other, jumped up and down and squealed some more. It seemed like the biggest accomplishment in the world at that point. Granted we were only fourteen years old, so making it onto our high school cheerleading squad was really a big deal. She was my cheerleading buddy and we had a great time together. We laughed together, cried together, we were even humiliated together. At our high school, varsity cheerleading was the big deal. The junior varsity squad was the warm-up for varsity. It's like that at every high school I guess, but it was really important for me to be a cheerleader because cheerleading meant status. My aunt was also a varsity cheerleader and she spent her summer helping me prepare for the tryouts, so I hated to think I could have let her down.

Only varsity cheerleaders cheered at the Friday night games because they were the more skilled cheerleaders. The JV squad had a whole other schedule that mostly only parents and friends attended. Freshmen and sophomore year, Kenz and I put in hard work on JV so that we could be juniors on the varsity team like most girls are. But a new coaching staff came in, and despite all of our hard work, neither of us could tumble. I could do a standard cartwheel, so could she, but none of that impressive forward-back-hand-spring-flapjack-air-attack stuff. A lot of heart - not a ton of tumbling skill. So that time, when we walked up to the door, we were happy to even have our names on the list but heartbroken that we would be third-year JV's, and even worse, that sophomores had been placed ahead of us. It stung. I had cheered for ten years straight, and I was ready to quit. I had sat on the bleachers at the Friday night games for two years and I thought that junior year I would be finally joining in. I was worried that I would be made fun of again - for not being enough. McKenzie almost quit, too. She was just as mad and embarrassed as I was. We were the only juniors on JV, but the coach did name us captains, which was nice of her. When a few of the cheerleaders got caught out partying hard and got in trouble with the police, or someone was sick or injured, we were the fill-ins for varsity, so we got to go to some of the games and cheer. It was hard though. We were good enough to be fill-ins when needed, but not good enough to actually be on the team. Kenz quit after that.

Senior year, I made it on to varsity, but it wasn't the same without Kenz. I really missed having her around. She was my buddy and it wasn't the same without her. Aside from cheerleading, Kenz and I went through a lot together. I actually witnessed her unravel in front of me. It was one of the most horrific things I have ever seen a friend endure.

Our senior year of high school though we didn't cheer together, we were still very close. Kenz's boyfriend of over a year cheated on her, with a girl we both knew (she and I cheered together, we were friends but not close friends, we became closer friends actually after high school then we were when we were in it). When Kenz found out that her boyfriend, who was the love of her life at that time, had cheated on her, she had a breakdown. It was in the middle of the school day, right before lunch was about to end when she found out. She was in no condition to go back and sit in a classroom, so she rushed to the guidance counselor's office as a safe haven. I was concerned so with her permission, I accompanied her. As she explained to the counselor what had happened, I held her hand. I could feel her entire body quivering, though she was not yet crying outside, it was as if there was a thunderstorm inside of her – crackling, shaking her very core. The guidance counselor was there to offer encouraging sentiments and suggest that perhaps Kenz and the girl should speak face to face. Hesitantly, Kenz agreed.

She wanted to know the truth. The guidance counselor called the girl into her office. When the girl came in, all of us were sitting. The counselor closed the door. I watched Kenz calm the storm inside of her (it reminded me a lot of a tactic mentioned using in 8th grade). Boldly, and courageously she stood up, letting go of my hand McKenzie appeared as tall and grand as a skyscraper.

Fiercely and consumed with rage, she asked the girl, "did you and Nate sleep together?"

When the girl didn't say anything, McKenzie repeated herself in a roar, "DID YOU AND NATE SLEEP TOGETHER?"

I had never heard her voice so loud or powerful.

The girl looked shamefully at the ground and responded… "yes".

With an even louder voice than before McKenzie screamed: "get out!". The girl left quickly and shut the door behind her. With the door shutting, Kenz dropped to the floor and curled into a ball. She looked like a skyscraper crumbling down to the ground. Appearing to be nothing but rubble. She hugged her knees, and she cried so hard she started hyperventilating. I didn't know how to help, the image stunned me at first, but then I dropped to the ground and held her in my arm, trying to hold her together. She shook and when the shaking got worse, I held her tighter as if I was trying to keep her from shattering all at once.

I was seventeen years old when that happened to her. I'm twenty-one now, and that is still one of the most devastating things I have ever witnessed. Because of that, I can't help but associate love with heartache. She and Nate seemed to have such a good relationship. He was the last guy I would have ever thought to do that to his girlfriend, but it still happened. I close my eyes, and I think of her small body, lying weakly on the ground, sobbing into the guidance counselor's carpet and it still breaks my heart.

If you were wondering, McKenzie is doing great now. We don't see each other nearly as much as we used to but she is on track to graduate next spring with a Biology degree. She is dating a guy that seems to make her really happy. That makes me really happy

for her. I know in real life, people don't always get
happy endings wrapped up in pretty little bows, but I
sure hope she gets one.

With love always,

Delilah

<u>McKenzie's Playlist</u>

Super Bass – Nicki Minaj

Louie Louie – The Kingsmen

Hey! Baby – Bruce Channel

Fifteen – Taylor Swift

Thunder – Boys Like Girls

Firework – Katy Perry

Schuyler's Chapter

Hello Confidant,

It was hard to decide where exactly to play Schuyler in this story. If I was being 100% chronological, Schuyler would go at the very beginning because we've been best friends since I was five and he was seven. Our moms are also best friends - the root of our friendship. Even as children, we had a chemistry between us. He was my first kiss when I was five. It was kind of foreshadowing our future relationship.

We were around each other a lot until middle school. After that, we didn't talk as much. We both got caught up in everything that was going on in our own lives - he had soccer, I had cheerleading and theatre and our parents got caught up in our hobbies, and with Schuyler and I going to separate schools so he and I drifted apart.

It wasn't until my freshman year of high school that I ran into him again at a wrestling match. We reminisced a little. That evening at home, I realized how much I missed having Schuyler around. He must have missed me too because as I was thinking about him, he texted me. We started talking more than we ever had before. A month later, that darling Charles cheated on me and Schuyler was my shoulder to cry on. He was the person to tell me that I deserved better. He was right - I did. At first, I thought he was being friendly and supportive, but nearly a week later he confessed that he had feelings for me and that he wanted to date me. When he said he liked me, it kind of threw me for a loop. He was almost like family, but there was a deeper attraction there that had not been present before. He has always been cute. And he was nice to me. And he made me feel special and giddy. I can tell when someone was just filling my head with pretty things, but Schuyler's words, advice, comments, they all seemed so romantic and thoughtful. So I said, "yeah let's go for it".

The first time we hung out was January 28, 2012. We went to a party together. He took a picture of me and put it on Facebook (and that's how I really knew he liked me). We were pretty much magnets the whole time. Even though we were at a party, it was him and I talking, locked together. On the way home from the party, he sat in the back seat with me. It was so dark that I could only see the outline of him. While

I was studying him, I felt his hand land on my leg. It felt warm. He then moved his hand up my thigh, up my hip, torso, chest, and then cheek. I turned toward him and he passionately kissed me. It wasn't at all like that kiss we had when we were five and seven years old. It was a real "I like you", "I want you" kiss. After that night we continued to hang out, he asked me to his Winter Ball, and I said yes. On school days, we FaceTimed in the evening and texted a lot. Our relationship was 50% of us being goo-goo gaga over each other and then 50% of us making fun of each other (in the best way). In reality, it was 100% infatuation. Then, he started talking to me about passion... physical passion. He talked about making love in a way that reminded me that we had been best friends our whole lives. He really cared about me and we had a history. With Charles things never felt natural. When it came to Schuyler, I could not help but think if I was going to lose my virginity to someone, who better it be than my best friend who I was now practically in a relationship with? I decided I wanted it to be him. I told him that I did not want it to be premeditated, though. If it was going to happen for us, it needed to be natural.

On Valentine's Day, he came over to my house and surprised me with flowers. My parents weren't home and wouldn't be for a long while. I let them know that Schuyler was coming over, so they said only stay in the living room. We went to my bedroom when he got there. I felt guilty for that later on - but it was in the moment thing and sometimes impulses take over, especially at fourteen. We started kissing, one thing led to another and ... dot, dot, dot. It happened. It was good. But not what I expected? I mean, movies... like *Dear John*, and *The Last Song*, they paint sex to be this magical, mystical, violin orchestra, 4th of July fireworks display and it just isn't, or at least it hasn't been for me. Ever. When it happened with Schuyler, I thought I had done something wrong because I didn't feel magical afterward. I felt like myself. No different - I mean a little sweaty but that was it. When Schuyler left, I called Marie because I had to tell her and I needed to talk to her about how I felt. I felt really, really weird. She has two older sisters that talked to her about sex, so even though she hadn't had it yet, I thought she might be able to fix my dilemma or at least I don't know, I needed someone to help me and tell me what I was feeling was normal. By the time I got Marie on the phone, my parents were home so I wanted to talk

quietly but still convey everything I was feeling.
During our conversation, my mom screamed "Delilah"!
And I thought "oh shit... she heard me. I'm dead.
d.e.a.d. dead." I told Marie I would be right back
and I ran to the top of the steps. Mom said "Schuyler
got in an accident on his way home. I'm meeting him
there until his mom can get there. Do you want to
come with me?". I was petrified. I nodded yes,
grabbed my slippers because they were my closest
shoes, told Marie I would call her back and then out
the door we went. I felt tears filling my eyes. We
didn't know what condition he was in. And after
everything that had happened between us, I was sure I
loved him. I didn't want to lose him. When we got to
Schuyler, his car was teetering on the side of a
cliff on a turn, but he was already sitting in the
ambulance. I felt relieved but still seriously
concerned. I walked over to him and asked if he was
okay. He looked angry. Like really angry. After his
car accident, he was not as cozy as he had previously
been with me. But I gave him a pass, I figured he was
upset that it had happened.

The winter ball was the following weekend. I had
the perfect white dress (because of
winter...snow...white. I thought that was what people

wore, but I found out they were dresses of all colors). When I got to his house to take pictures for the snowball dance, he hardly looked at me. He didn't compliment me. He barely touched me. I thought maybe it was because our parents were standing around with us. After that, we went out to dinner. On the car ride there, he still didn't hold my hand or touch me, or ANYTHING. At dinner, I felt the most awkward. He went to a different school than me so I didn't know anyone else but him at the table. There were six of us in the group, myself included and he said maybe three words to me the entire time we were at dinner. By now, I was feeling sad and confused.

At the ball, we danced together but without really making eye contact. Then the first slow song of the night came on, "I Don't Want to Miss a Thing" by Aerosmith. He spun me around and pulled me in to dance. I rested my head on his shoulder, and things started to feel okay. I wasn't as nervous. I felt happier. More at peace. I lifted my head up off of his shoulder and looked at him. I kept thinking how handsome he was...then I noticed he wouldn't make eye contact with me. He hadn't the entire evening. He hadn't really since after we had sex... then I started to think, was it the car accident that had

made him upset? Or did he blame me for the car
accident? Or was the sex really bad? All of these
things started flickering through my head. I started
to feel like I was going to throw up. I kept my
composure though and tried my best to look like I was
still having a good time.

After the dance, his mom drove me home. He rode
in the car with me, and he sat in the back seat with
me, but it felt unnatural. When we pulled up to my
house, I thanked his mom for the ride and got out. I
heard her say "Schuyler, you better get out of the
car and walk her up", and then she said "I'm going to
come in and talk to her mom for a second", but by
then I was already halfway up the sidewalk and I
quickly walked into the house without even saying
hello to my family. I ran up the steps to my bedroom.
I tore off my dress, brushed out my hair, I felt like
crying but I didn't. I could hear our moms talking
downstairs, ever so often I could hear him make a
comment. I put on comfy clothes and walked back
downstairs, trying to appear cool, calm, and
collected. I thanked Schuyler for taking me and gave
him a hug. Our moms cooed at us together. And then he
left. I felt a weird, empty feeling inside. I pushed
it away and decided to lay down and watch TV. While I

was laying there, I got a text on my phone... from Schuyler. I saw his name flash across the screen and I got excited. I thought he was going to tell me how much he liked me or that he had a nice time, instead his message read, "I'm sorry but I don't think this is going to work out", tears filled my eyes. I played it off. I replied "Oh, okay. Why's that?", and said "I just don't, ttyl" that was it. I was devastated. It was one disappointment after another. First Charles, then Schuyler. I wanted that magical feeling to last with someone. What was I doing wrong? I scanned my memory of Valentine's Day night, and I wondered if it was something I did then, and I went through my memories of the week after Valentine's Day, and the night of the dance and I had no idea what I did wrong. I still don't.

Eventually, a year later to be exact, he texted me to see how I was doing. I didn't get an explanation from him until the summer of 2014 when our families went on a cruise together. He texted me the day of the cruise and said "Can't wait to see you, when are you getting on?" like nothing had happened between us. But I figured if he could let it go, then I should too. We casually hung out together. Me, him, my brother, and his sister. We went out at night together, we played mini-golf on the sky deck. Then one night, he asked me if I wanted to go walk around the sky deck... and I said "sure!", I was dating a guy at the time, and Schuyler was with a girl in a very serious relationship, so there were no romantic intentions involved. It was only he and me at the top of the cruise ship with the ocean wind blowing on us. At first, we talked about our recent endeavors, and then we talked about our goals and aspirations... it was the summer before my senior year so he asked me where I wanted to go after, and then we talked about his career in the military. He told me how hard it was for him and that there were times when he would go into the stall and weep because it was so hard. I felt sad for him. But then I got really angry. I blurted out "why did you do that to me?", and he looked dumbfounded and he said "do what?", and I said, "why did you lead me on, have sex with me and then completely drop me?", and he responded, "I was a stupid, immature kid, I didn't know what I was doing but I am sorry" ... He apologized and it was sincere. Like actually sincere. We hugged it out and we were good. We had a nice time on the rest of the trip together.

To this day, every once in a while we check in on each other but our relationship will always be complicated. He is in the military so he lives far away. It's hard to be friends with someone you've had intimate relationships with. But he has been around for a long time... and he always will be. There is a special place in my heart for him. I do love him in some way. Despite everything that has happened between us, he is one of the most reliable men that I have in my life.

With love always,

Delilah

<u>Schuyler's Playlist</u>

Mary's Song — Taylor Swift

Clean — Taylor Swift

Stay — Rihanna

Jar of Hearts — Christina Perri

Cool — Gwen Stefani

Liam's Chapter

Hello Confidant,

After things went downhill with me and Schuyler, I was very weak, very shaken, and very vulnerable…and I had not really learned from my mistakes. I kept wondering why I wasn't striking gold. Well, it was because I hadn't been paying attention to everything I was doing wrong.

There was a man who showed interest in me, please remember I was only fourteen at the time. He was nineteen. We had five years in between us, but I was attracted to him because of his maturity, because of his stability, and we shared a common interest of theatre (I thought that's what I needed after all of the bad luck with guys I had experienced, someone who was mature).

Liam understood me or so I thought. I won't go to details, I don't want to go into details. What you need to know is I got very drunk at a party and I made some mistakes. Two weeks after my mistakes, Liam decided that I was too young for him and he started dating a girl one year older than me. In a matter of one month I felt like I was spiraling out of control.

That's when I met Justin.

Confidant, I am telling you this because you must understand if a change is what you desire, look at your mistakes. Your old ways won't allow you to grow, you will remain stunted for as long as you choose to be. It is a choice — that's the secret that everyone forgets to tell you.

With love always,

Delilah

We've Got A Big Mess On Our Hands - The Academy Is

Justin's Chapter

Hello Confidant,

I know that a lot happened in those sections back there and they happened very fast. If you're still with me at this point, I hope you're not judging me and I hope you're not judging any of the other people either. Because all of the people I'm talking about in this book, they're just that – people. People make mistakes. People are selfish. People are stupid. People are *human*. Humans are flawed. Even some of the most spectacular figures in history have made mistakes – it's *human* nature. If you're going to stay with me, and continue on this journey I need you to keep that in mind because it's not fair for you to judge these people who you've never met.

Maybe right now you're questioning me, and you're asking yourself "why is she even writing this if she doesn't want us to judge people?" and the answer is:

I just want to share my pain and my happiness with all of you because maybe someone somewhere out there might pick this up and read it, and maybe they've experienced something like I have and they'll know they aren't alone.

Maybe there is something in this that you can relate to, and if that's the case please know that you're not alone. That's why I want to tell this story. I've never been a victim. I won't ever be a victim. I am a storyteller.

I'm glad we got that cleared up. Now onto Justin

Justin came into my life at a very weird time. Charles hurt me, Schuyler hurt me, and then there was, of course, Liam physically and then mentally screwed me. I was in an awful place.

I saw auditions for a local play was coming up and it had almost been a year since I had been in a show. With a headstrong mindset kicking back in, I started putting all of my energy into preparing an audition song and trying to heal. The show was in the next town over but I expressed to my mother how much I wanted to be in it. She supports me. She has always supported my dreams, so she shuttled my butt over to the other town and let me audition. This was before my self-confidence had started building back up so I was a little shy in my audition and I could've given it more but I didn't and that was my own damn fault. I didn't get a lead role but I was one of the supporting characters.

While I was auditioning I noticed a boy in the crowd, he was cute. I introduced myself to him and found out his name was Justin. We both got into the show and he was the leading male character.

Justin and I had instant chemistry. We flirted back and forth at rehearsals a lot. He was a little dorky but in a cute way. I kept going for guys with big egos and he was cute, but he didn't know it. I wanted him to know it and I wanted to be the girl to make him realize it. Feeling brave, one day after rehearsal I asked him if he would like to rehearse together, he asked me where and I said something like maybe the mall and we could grab pizza, and then he said "are you sure you wouldn't want to just go on a date?" so then we went on a date. After a couple of dates, we decided we were a couple. Justin was that nice guy that I had been looking for. And when I say nice, I mean nice. He always opened the door for me. He was so respectful. Kind. He would send me the sweetest message to brighten my day. I could tell that he was the kind of guy who didn't use girls. He was a big sweetheart.

The show we were in together happened to land on my birthday weekend so the night before my birthday, he insisted that the entire cast go out to eat and wait until midnight so that everyone could sing me "happy birthday". On my actual birthday, which we had a performance on, he showed up with a present and flowers. The present he got me was a necklace with a quote about me being a beautiful person inside and out.

He was so sweet, he had the sweetest family, and I was happy with him for about three months and then I let my little monster, Betty, fucking Betty, ruin my happiness. Betty said to me "you don't deserve him, he's a nice guy and you're going to hurt him. You aren't as in this as he is" and then sometimes that little monster would also say "he's not really a nice guy, the rug is going to come up from you, he is going to hurt you like everyone else did don't fall too hard." And just like that, that voice inside my head got so loud that I couldn't block it out any longer. I got scared and I knew I had to end things.

Even though I finally got that sweet guy I wanted, I couldn't get over my own crap. I didn't want to keep someone around who would've had to deal with that. I decided that I needed to be by myself for a little while. Justin was devastated. I remember hearing his voice crack as I explained myself and I hated hurting him. It hurt me. After that, I was done with romance/dating/boys/all of the above. I got asked out on dates by people, some of them were really nice guys but I needed a healing time. Justin was one of the sweetest guys I've ever dated to this day. I know he cared about me a lot and I cared about him too but I had to care about me more. That's selfish. However, sometimes you need to be selfish because you have to come first to you and I was in a place filled with self-doubt and sadness and I needed to stand on my own and be a whole person by myself. If you don't love yourself completely, with all of your wonders and your flaws, you cannot expect anyone else to love you. At that point in time, I didn't love myself at all. I actually hated who I was and I was embarrassed by it. I was embarrassed that I kept falling down and getting back up and then being shoved down again and then getting back up and then getting hurt over and over again. It was devastating.

Being selfish was necessary. It helped me to heal. It took dating a good guy and still not feeling whole to make me realize what I needed. I needed to be around friends and people that loved me without expecting anything out of me.

Justin and I remain friends after everything because he was a good guy and he got it. Justin is still pursuing theatre. He is passionate and his passion and optimism will take him really places. One day he is going to make someone very happy.

With love always,

Delilah

Sweet Dreams Interlude

I don't trust boys who don't say "sweet dreams". That's the nicest thing you could wish upon someone before they go to sleep. A simple "good night" does not cut it.

With love always,

Delilah

Cut Interlude

Hello Confidant,

There are some relationships that just didn't make the cut into this.

They were important at the time, but not relevant enough for mentioning.

Funny.

I wasn't relevant enough for them to make the relationship work.

Now they aren't relevant enough for me to do more than vaguely elude to on this very page.

With love always,

Delilah

Doubt's Chapter

Hello Confidant,

I had a dream last night that all of the boys who had ever hurt me formed a club and burned my book.

But I smiled because...

In order for them to have burned my book, they had to buy my book.

I still win.

With love always,

Delilah

A's Chapter

(Alternative Heading: Baby's First Heartbreak)

(A love story so tragic, I used his real name. You're welcome.)

Alright, so you have heard about some of my almost loves. Out of everyone who has hurt me, this guy has hurt me the very most. I put my trust in him. I started making long-term plans with him. I don't think he really ever saw me as more than someone to pass the time with. "Brace yourself," is something I wish someone had told me when I first laid eyes on him, "this love is going to hurt you". My first real love shattered my heart into a million pieces. I loved him with every fiber of my being; anything I could have done for that guy, I would have. He said he loved me, but words without actions are hard to back up.

How we met:

Just kidding….

Backstory:

Marie's mother taught high school in a neighboring county. One time Marie and A actually met, and when they met she told me that he and I would be perfect together. I passed the notion along thinking "when will I ever meet someone from (insert town here), it's an hour away!" Anyways, they remained friends.

NOW how we met:

The summer in between my sophomore and junior year of high school I went to "HOBY" (The Hugh O'Brian Youth Leadership Program), a seminar where budding high school juniors attended the conference to learn more about building positive environments and being better leaders in our community. The people who attended "HOBY" were mostly very nice people. Upon arrival, we got divided into groups, I was put into the group "I". I made fast friends with some of the girls there, we still talk to this very day. Every time I see one of them out somewhere, we hug and we catch up. Some of the other Group I members still message me and root for me on a day to day basis. I made quality friends from being in Group I. While doing some group icebreakers, I noticed this guy looking at me like he knew me, but I had no clue who he was. During a break, he came up to me and said "You're Delilah, Marie's friend! I've watched your videos on YouTube. You're such an incredible singer. I'm A." I was beyond flattered. We started talking to get to know each other better. During the next presentation, he sat beside me. When I would raise my hand to answer a question, he would jokingly raise his hand higher than me and say to me "I know the right answer, you don't". He liked to tease me that way.

Our group spent the day together, but A was like my best friend instantly. He was smart, attractive, and he had a good style; he was really smooth. I developed a little bit of a crush on him because he was not at all like the guys I was used to meeting back home. He had a level of sophistication about him that I found captivating, but I reminded myself that we had just met and that we lived an hour away from each other, it would never really work out.

Our group had dinner together. Then at the dance that night we hung out some, but I mostly danced with my girlfriends. I was there to grow as a leader and make friends.

The next morning at breakfast, he greeted by the cafeteria door with a big smile on his face and said "Good morning sunshine, how did you sleep? Let's all have breakfast together." I blushed, I responded with an easy going response, and then some of my new friends, some of A's friends, and then myself and A all had breakfast together. At the following lecture, we sat next to each other and flirted a lot. Then at one of the seminars the next day, I saw a hair tie on his wrist and he didn't have long enough hair to pull his up. It was his girlfriend's hair tie; he wore it on his wrist for whatever reason. As I was already developing feelings for him, I decided it was best to stop the flirting and be normal with him, not all giddy. Except, I didn't tell him about my decision, or realizing he was with somebody, I started acting cold. A few moments later, he was trying to play footsies with me, I leaned over and told him to stop, he asked "why?", and I said "I don't think your girlfriend would like that. I wouldn't if it were me." He smiled a little, he had been caught and he looked guilty, and yet he was still very charming.

After the seminar ended our group leader told us that there was a talent show happening that night, and then asked everyone if they had any talents. I

was shy about singing in front of people, so I
decided to shake my head "no", as in I didn't have
any talents. But then A piped up and said "Delilah
can sing! Look here is a video from YouTube", and
then everyone was like oh you have to sing! I looked
at him with a face full of frustration, and he smiled
at me. I couldn't turn down a whole group of people
rooting for me to perform, and he knew that. That
night when I got up on stage, I sang "Hey Ho" by the
Lumineers. The crowd sang along, and it was a truly
happy moment – one of my favorites in fact. After I
finished singing, I heard people's voices cheering my
full name. It was led by A (his voice was very
recognizable and the loudest one cheering). As soon
as I got off the stage, he hugged me and he told me
that he was proud of me. It made me really happy. He
and I danced together that night at the seminar's
dance. It was sweet, and I got very caught up in my
feelings and then the reminder that he had a
girlfriend snapped me out of it. With my head resting
on his shoulder, I started to pull away but he placed
his hand in the center and leaned in closer to ask me
what was wrong. I told him I had been cheated on
before, and I couldn't contribute to it. Though the
feelings that I was feeling came on really fast, they
were so real. He told me he was going to end things

with her- he had made that decision before meeting me. He continued on about how they didn't have a serious relationship together, she was two years older than him, and it was a casual thing. They had played soccer together, and they were dating but they weren't really involved. I told him that I understood, but as long as there was someone else in the picture I couldn't be.

The next day, our group was sent to repair The Boys and Girls club as our act of volunteer work. A and I were painting a door together in one of the classrooms, and the rest of our group had disappeared into the other room. He started singing as he was painting, it made me smile. Then all of the sudden, our hands brushed against each other. I looked over at him, he looked at me. There could have been a kiss. But there wasn't. Both of us wanted to, neither of us initiated it. I couldn't be close to him anymore, I felt guilty. At dinner that night, we didn't sit beside each other. However, I noticed that there was no hair tie on his wrist. I didn't comment on it. That evening, I was standing by the glass doors near the lobby while another dance took place, and A walked up and stood beside me. He said, "look", and pointed at the window. I didn't know what I was looking for, so I looked hard out of the window. Then, he said "look how good we look together." and pointed at our reflections. I blushed and he took my hair tie off of my wrist and put it on his. I was smitten. When "HOBY" ended, I never really expected to hear from him again. I figured it was an in the moment thing. Before I went to bed that night, I made my peace with everything that had happened between us and then I let it go. I fell asleep in my own bed and slept really well.

The next morning when I woke up I had a trillion texts from A. He professed his feelings to me; he was in love with me, too. He broke it off with the girl as soon as he got home and he wanted us to be together. It felt really good to read those texts. He wanted me, the same way I wanted him.

I told him that I didn't want our relationship to start via a text conversation. I wanted to test the waters with him a bit before we got too invested. He then began writing me love letters. Every other day I had a letter in the mail from him. One of them requesting for me to be his girlfriend. I said yes. We started dating on June 18th. We were both attending more summer academies, so we didn't get the chance to see each other before school started back up. Then his school played mine in a soccer match and I finally got to see him again. When I saw him at the field, the moment I saw him, he was already smiling. His smile made me so weak. It was one of those love at first sight cases. The moment we met, he made me feel different than anyone ever had.

After "HOBY", we dated for two years. We didn't see each other a lot, but we FaceTimed every day and texted all the time. He came to my junior homecoming, and prom, and my senior homecoming. We had movie dates, we saw each other at sporting events (our first kiss was actually at my brother's football game). When I took my driving test, he even showed up at the DMV to cheer me on. The distance was hard, but we felt like we were soul mates so we made it work. Sometimes we had FaceTime movie dates where we would both watch a movie together so we could feel like we were on a date. Anytime I was having a bad day, he would find a way to fix it for me, and I did the same for him. We talked about anything and everything. I became so comfortable with him. I genuinely thought that he was the person I married. Despite what happened with the guys before A, I still believed in love. I was in a really healthy place mentally, too, which I thought meant that I was ready to receive it. Sometimes I got scared that with the long-distance relationship, that when we did get around each other, things would be awkward, but we always managed to pick right back where we left off. We spent one night together, at his house. His parents weren't home, so he had me come over. When I got to his place, he had dinner for me, and then we watched a movie together before falling asleep in one another's arms. When I woke up in the morning to him next to me, I felt not only happiness but comfort. From the moment I met that man, it felt as though I had known him my whole life. While we were dating, people asked me how I managed to do the whole long-distance relationship type thing. I confessed it was hard, but I thought he was my person.

I wasn't going to talk about the bad with him, though he hurt me, as my first love I wanted to only remember the good…but then a few months ago I came across one of his tweets. It said something along the lines of marrying your high school sweetheart was like only trying vanilla ice cream and then deciding that was the only good flavor. Being his high school sweetheart, it really upset me and it launched me into this thought: Am I really just vanilla to some people? It hurt me almost as much as him cheating on me after I put mountains of trust and love into our relationship. Three years have almost past since one nasty break up with A. A break up that should have happened probably a year before it did. In the privacy of this wonderful little space, I can elaborate.

The first time I have ever felt anger, intense anger happened while I was dating A. The date was June 4th, 2014 (two weeks' shy of our one-year anniversary) when this unpleasant little series of events began. The week before I had gone on my first ever cruise, with my family, to the Bahamas. On the cruise, was the first man I ever had sex with, who you met in Chapter 3, Schuyler. As I mentioned, he was a family friend, and despite our personal encounter, he remained a friend of mine for years after and still is a friend to this very day. There were a few times when we were alone together when something could have happened, however, both of us were in relationships with people who we thought we were going to be spending our whole lives with. Both of us were wrong. I was seventeen, he was nineteen. We didn't know how cruel people who say they "love you" can actually be. What I am saying here is nothing happened. I did not even have to fight an urge because during my vacation the only person I thought about was my darling boyfriend with whom I was totally goo-goo gaga, starry-eyed over. Without A's goodnight and good morning phone calls, my heart felt empty despite all the fun I was having on vacation. During the cruise, I spent $15 on an email telling him that I loved and missed him (I definitely deserve Venmoed back for that). What sucked the most is when I got back to the US, he was leaving on a separate cruise for another whole week, which meant two weeks without any communication for us, other than that mere Sunday when we both had cell reception.

To occupy my mind, and time, I had my best friend, Marie, over. She and I did home projects for my bedroom, hung out, listened to music, the norm. I also worked a lot. I enjoyed working where I did. It was a hometown pizza store. My family was friends with the family who owned it, people I knew came in all the time, though it was fun it was also busy. So on June 4th, 2014, I worked from 10 AM - 10 PM, a long, greasy shift. I got home, and immediately put my clothes in the washing machine, and took a long, hot shower to wash the smell of pizza and grease off of me. When I got out of the shower, I noticed I had a pending message on Facebook from a guy saying that the person I loved was cheating me with this guy's girlfriend. At that time, I felt so many emotions at once, confusion, frustration, betrayal, heartbreak (for the first time ever), and optimism. I cried. I cried so hard, but quietly because I did not want to wake up my mom who was sleeping in the next room.

I called Marie, and she came over. We talked, and I decided that I would have a little more faith in A. I desperately needed to talk to him, but he did not have any service out in the middle of the ocean, so I had to have faith and patience. The next day, Marie and I went to my grandparent's pool, and as I was about to get into the pool I got a text message from A. I fell to my knees as soon as I got it. I felt such relief. He said that this boy was a liar, and jealous of a friendship that A had with this guy's girlfriend. He told me that he would never to do anything to hurt me, that he loved me, and would talk to me soon. That was enough for me. He had never done anything to hurt me before, so my suspicions, my fears were settled and the heartache faded away to me just missing him.

When he got back from his vacation, we both agreed we desperately needed to see each other. We missed one another and we need to celebrate our one-year anniversary. I dressed to impress; I put on my favorite hot pink dress. Marie drove us to a town near his where we went to the movie theatre with my love, and one of his guy friends. Afterward, we went to a scenic overlook (one I still visit time to time), and we sat and held hands, and kissed, and laughed. I felt so in love, and so lucky. The forty-five-minute car ride home, I cried at first, because I hated for the date to be over. I loved him so much but I knew dealing with the long distance was worth waiting for a lifetime of happiness with him. The rest of the drive back, Marie and I talked about what kind of future I saw with him and I saw it clear as a day. There were some complications such as our college selections, but we did the long-distance thing, and four more years in college compared to a lifetime together seemed agreeable. I was also very optimistic that we would pick the same school. We got back to my house, and my friend and I kept talking. In that conversation, I started mentioning sacrificing some of my dreams to accommodate things such as his residency (he wanted to be a doctor). It was at that moment that my best friend stopped me from talking and said, "before you go on anymore. I can't not tell you this. I asked his friend about the situation last week, and he said all he could say to me was 'it's hard because I am caught between being a good person and being a good friend'." As soon as she said that me, my love high vanished, I felt pain again my heart and a sadness that hit me like a cruise ship.

I asked A once more if he had anything to tell me. He confessed to it. He had been involved with that other guy's girlfriend. A told me that nothing actually happened; that he just crossed some boundaries with some of the things that he said to her. It hurts my feelings, but he promised it would stop and that it would never happen again and I loved him with all of my heart. I didn't want to lose him, but I already had.

We stayed together almost a year more, but then things eventually fizzled out and died. Ironically enough, as soon as we broke up, he started dating the girl he cheated on me with. He had perfect timing, too. The day he decided to call it quits was two days before my 18th birthday, and two weeks before my senior prom. His cheating, his timing, his selfishness… that was what made me question if he ever loved me. I would have gone to the ends of the Earth for that boy but he didn't reciprocate my feelings. He was selfish and spoiled and too caught up in himself to really care about anyone else. He faked it so well though.

Last summer, he was in town for the months of June and July, living only ten minutes away from me. He asked for us to see each other, but I couldn't see him. The thought of seeing him out somewhere terrifies me because I have no idea how I would react. I don't know if I would be normal, or burst into tears. It is scary for one person to have so much emotional power over another human being.

I thought I had felt heartbreak before with other guys when it didn't work out. In truth, I did not know what love was until I met A. The entire first half of our relationship felt like I was walking around with stars in my eyes. So in love. so happy, so sure that he was my person, so naive.

Real heartbreak never goes away. The type of betrayal I felt from him haunts me to this day. In my other relationships, I wrongly compare them to my first love. The second things start getting serious with someone, I write it off as implausible. I struggle to believe in a future with anyone. The second I start to think long-term, I run away from it. The toll that the relationship took on me, has been something I can't seem to get away from. Other guys might have hurt me, but A broke my heart. He betrayed my trust. He made my view on the world darker, skewed, and skeptic. I don't think he loved me. You can't do that to someone you love. Also, high school (sweet)hearts are only vanilla if you make them only vanilla. My high school sweetheart was rocky road, and I do not eat ice cream anymore. In fact, I am lactose intolerant.

With love always,

Delilah

A's Playlist

Ho Hey – The Lumineers

Collide – Jake Miller

Fallin' – The Lumineers

Still Into You – Paramore

Kiss Me – Ed Sheeran

Stubborn Love – The Lumineers

Stay the Night – Zedd

Mirrors- Justin Timberlake

First Flight Home – Jake Miller

If I Were A Boy – Beyoncé

Somebody That I Used to Know – Gotye

Molly – Lil Dicky

Hey There Delilah – Plain White T's

Sweet Disappointment's Chapter

I have always wanted to live in New York City. The Big Apple. That's the place where I wanted to end up right after high school. With that being said, my obvious dream school was none other a university in NYC - NYU, Tisch specifically. I went to my auditions for the school with my grandmother. The night before the audition, she took me to see Wicked so that I would be inspired for my audition. I was. It worked. When I auditioned - I sang two songs that best displayed my voice but at that time I didn't realize I wanted to study Acting more than Musical Theatre. See, musical theatre is a triple threat. I have a decent singing voice, I'm good at acting, but dancing - whew… well let's say I have taken some classes since then and I think, I think I might possibly know what rhythm is now… but then not so much. I was hopeful, though, that they might still pick me, or see something special in me.

On the night that admissions letters were sent out, I waited up all night. I couldn't sleep because I was far too busy playing out all of the possible scenarios in my head: getting accepted and moving to my dream place, or getting denied and having to figure all of that out. It was exhausting so one would think that I would have been out like a light, but I could not bring myself to rest. I drowned myself in the Mamma Mia soundtrack. I wished and hoped and begged and pleaded that I would be accepted. I even wore my cozy, purple NYU hoodie for good luck.

At six a.m., I still had no letter declaring my fate and I had school to get ready for. Mustering up as much energy as I possibly could, I pulled on a pair of leggings and got ready for my day. My eyes felt like they were blistering from being awake so long, but my hopes were high.

Ten minutes before I had to leave, the admission letter found its way to my inbox. It went a little something like "we regret to inform you…" you get it. I was denied. Crushed. I was crushed.

With "Dancing Queen" playing in the background, I looked at myself in the mirror. I was young and sweet, and only seventeen but I felt like a huge bag of garbage. I had an internal monologue: "Why did you think this was going to work out? Do you honestly think you even had a chance? How can I go to school

and face all of those people who think I'm ridiculous
for even dreaming of this in the first place?" I
inhaled deeply. And then exhaled loudly. (Try it,
right now. Experience it. It really is settling) I
grabbed my things and loaded into my mom's car. It
wasn't until after I got in the car that I realized I
had my NYU sweatshirt still on. Great. "Now I get to
look at that all day", I thought to myself. In the
car, I told my mom that I had been denied and she
said something like "that's okay sweetheart, it
would've been very expensive". I nodded. She was
right but it didn't matter. I was sad. Everything
felt heavy and bleak. A dream had died.

Walking down the hallway, I guess I didn't look
myself. One of my favorite teacher's, who always
stood in the hallway in the mornings to greet his
students. noticed right away, and he asked if I was
doing okay. I shrugged. I was afraid if I said it out
loud another time I would start crying and wouldn't
be able to stop. He stepped to the side and asked me
what the matter was. I said "I didn't get in" and
then pulled at my sweatshirt. He looked at me very
sympathetically and comfortingly put his hand on my
shoulder, and then very seriously said to me
"Delilah, New York will always be there waiting for

you. If that's where you want to be, you'll get there. It isn't the right time for you right now, but one day it will be. New York City isn't going anywhere." I smiled and I nodded. That was the first time I had smiled in the past twelve hours. His words reloaded my energy and made me hungry for better things to come. NYU didn't know me. NYU didn't believe in me…so what? So many other people did.

By not going to NYU, I met some of my very best friends and some other mentors that have drastically changed my world. They force me to be my best and push my limits. They bring out the best parts of me. I wish I could tell that young and sweet seventeen-year-old girl who felt as though her world was crumbling down around her, that in fact, dancing queen, it was barely even starting to grow.

With love always,

Delilah

Cheater, Cheater, Heart Eater's Chapter

One time I wrote this whole story about how it would turn out with me and this guy I barely knew. His name was Nolan.

Nolan wasn't extraordinarily handsome – he was extraordinarily tall and I was physically attracted to him, but we didn't always connect mentally or emotionally. He had a very neutral way about him.

We had been flirting back and forth for a few weeks. We had a little in common. We both liked art and New York City. He seemed like the type of person I would date. After a while of simple texting, he asked me to come over to his apartment and so I did. When I got to his place, I found out he shared an apartment with three other guys and they were occupying the living room. He asked me if I would be okay hanging out in his room, and I agreed to. He led me to his room, I sat on the edge of his bed with my back to the wall, and he sat at the foot of the bed. There was discomfort being on his bed so casually. In that realm of awkwardness, we talked about a lot of different things such as *his* favorite sports teams, *his* lifestyle, *his* goals… We got on the subject of his last relationship, and how it ended – something that really peaked my interest! He confessed he had cheated on his previous girlfriend. A lot. As someone who had been cheated on, my first instinct was to ask him why he cheated on her, and so I did. He responded "I stopped caring about her feelings. We hit a rough patch and she got on my nerves so bad that I didn't want to be with her anymore. I tried to tell her that, but she wouldn't let go of it and tried to trap me in the relationship. So I started having sex with other girls, and when she found out, she finally let go of me."

While he continued to talk, I looked inward. I thought of how that poor girl must have felt. The more I thought about it, the more it made me angry. Girls who are emotional get bad names like "crazy" or "obsessive". But a boy does it to her. He leads her on.

He calls her beautiful.

Then suddenly...POOF! He is no longer interested.

He doesn't want to talk.

He doesn't want her to know where he is.

He doesn't care anymore.

And it all happens so fast, like lightning. Anyone would be confused and want answers after that.

That made me have a thought about cheating. Something I have always found peculiar about it is how quickly blame is placed on the unfamiliar party.

Picture this situation: Boy and girl#1 are together, boy cheats on girl #1 with girl #2. Girl #1 finds out, calls girl # 2 a "slut" (a very ugly word, IMO), and then forgives boy, but girl # 2 actually didn't even know about girl #1 and girl #1 is vigorously hating on girl #2, who did not or have any personal connection to girl #1.

What I mean to say is, when someone cheats the other person in the relationship is so quick to be angry at the third party person when it is their significant other who they should be angry with. That other person doesn't fill their ears with lies and false promises.

Nothing makes me angrier than that. If your significant other is a cheater, and you want to work past it fine. But put the blame on the appropriate person.

Also, it is 2018. Do not slut shame. You have no idea what that person has endured. Everyone and I mean everyone, is fighting their own bloody uphill, battle. Be kind.

Looking back at this now… I should have left right then. But I sympathized with him… Why??? because of the physical attraction? Our conversations continued for a little while after he mentioned cheating but nothing quite as interesting was said. After that, we stopped talking. He was a red flag. I finally got better at spotting those… or so I thought.

With love always,

Delilah

Heart Shaped Rose Colored Glasses
Interlude

Call me a hopeless romantic, call me an idiot, I'll call myself optimistic. I wonder why I am so focused on:

a. love

b. love stories

c. all of the above

Then I am reminded that in order for the human race to thrive on (and yes we are thriving in a lot of ways; we practically live in The Jetson's era) then people MUST continue to believe in love and fall in love. Love leads to wanting babies, love helps makes babies (and true, sometimes vodka does too, but what if humanity runs out of potatoes?!). The Beatles were on to something when they sang "all you need is love".

As long as there is humanity, there will be love or the potential for it. It's a constant and that's comforting. To imagine a world without it is to imagine a world that is bleak and impossible. Love makes history. Love makes the world spin. If the moon did not love the Earth, we wouldn't be able to appreciate the stars…and a world without stars just seems strange. Does it not?

With love always,

Delilah

Jordan's and Tiff's Chapter

Hello Confidant,

Through everything, it has been my friends who have helped me survive. There is a special thing to be said about people who choose to enter your life and stick it out with you. They see your pretty, they see your ugly, but they love who you are and they don't mind those imperfect parts. That is the kind of friendship that I have with Tiff and Jordan. It was hard for me to make friends for a while because of my insecurities, but Jordan and Tiff don't care about insecurities - they love all of the sides of me.

Jordan, Tiff, and I started being friends the summer before our sophomore year college - we met in a show. After one of our shows, we went back to Jordan's house. In the car ride there, Jordan and I made small talk - the kind that you have when you first start really getting to know someone. Our conversations kept leveling up though; they took a deeper turn; we got onto the subject of relationships and lust and love and everything in between. I found that she and I shared views on a lot of things and we clicked. It is truly a magical feeling when that happens with another person. There was something in me that told me I could trust her.

The same thing happened with Tiff — that connection, a gut trusting feeling. Tiff was so open and honest. They both are so refreshingly honest and in a world full of bullshit — that's what I needed. Tiff and I connect on a different level than Jordan and I do, no less, no more, just different. Our conversations can be about anything topic known to man and we will still find a way to gab about it for hours.

They both support me. They both love me. I was really worried that after high school, I wouldn't be able to make quality friends, but I got so lucky with those two. They have helped me grow as a human. Thanks to them embracing me for who I am without judgment or hesitation, I have been able to push my social anxiety away. Doing so has brought more wonderful friendships into my life; I have a very lucky life. My garden is full.

With love always,

Delilah

A Snake Interlude

I saw a snake lying in a mangled way in my garden, crying for its life.

I tended it wounds, and comforted it as it wept. I healed it with my own devotion.

The moment I turned away from it, it sunk its fangs into my flesh and injected its venom into me.

A snake will always be a snake.

With love always,

Delilah

Zayne's Chapter

Hi Confidant,

More boy talk - happening right now. Are you ready? I'm going to talk about the guy I had a crush on for seven years. I never had the nerve to go up to him but then fate aligned everything and Zayne and I had an encounter at a time where we both single.

October (the first time)

We started talking to each other after not speaking with one another for about a year. We got caught up in school, but we were both attending the same school in the same town, and one way or another we stumbled into each other's lives. He was still devilishly handsome like I had remembered. I swooned. Our conversations were common getting to know one another better talks until they weren't anymore. They got intimate. I thought we were going to date, as in he was going to be my boyfriend, I would be his girlfriend, we would hold hands and take cute, teeth rotting pictures together. Negative. Between our busy schedules, we hardly had any time to make plans together but a miracle happened and we both had a free evening. I invited him over and he said that he couldn't wait. I was so excited for the date. I skipped all of my classes that day to clean my apartment (I scrubbed the woodwork with a toothbrush). I made baked ziti and made cookies (because that's what Cher did on *Clueless* when the boy came over). I lit candles. I shaved my legs. The place looked nice. I looked nice.

My roommate had work that evening so she wouldn't be home. It would just be Zayne and me. I had jitters and I was buzzing with excitement. As I was setting the table, I heard a noise from my phone. It was Zayne. He wasn't coming. He said, "I'm sorry but I think that we are looking for two different things here. I can't come over". I said something along the lines of "what do you mean?" and he said, "you're a relationship person, and I'm not looking for that. But if you ever want to have sex, let me know." WAIT WHAT? He stood you up, Delilah, and then asked you to sleep with him?! Yes. Yes, he did. I wish I could say our story ended there, but I would be telling a lie. Something about him made me weak – his eyes, his dark brown hair, his jawline? I have no clue… so that my dear, whoever you are, is why there was a second time.

January (the second time)

A common friend of ours (Zayne and myself), Jake, was having a birthday party. Tiff and Jordan were going to be in attendance, and I had made plans to go as well. I found out Zayne was going from Zayne himself. We had started talking again, not regularly but often enough. He told about some of his hopes and dreams; his passions. He talked to me normally, and then he would ask me questions about me (as if he was truly interested in knowing the answers). He and I had a lot in common: taste in music, hobbies, interests. The fact that he was coming back into my life made everything feel like it was supposed to happen. When I found he was going to be at the party I got so nervous. I put on a nice (semi-sexy) outfit and took the extra time to feel really pretty. When he walked in the door, I remember he was wearing a yellow sweatshirt, and he was already smiling. It was as if he knew as soon as he walked in the door that he had me. I took shot of vodka, after shot of vodka. Everything after him walking in the door I only remember in spots – think of a strobe light going, sometimes the light completely brightens out my memory (as in I have no idea what happened). Zayne and I sat on a couch drinking and talking, I was so drunk that I spilled my drink down the front of me. I bopped around and mingled with friends. Zayne came up to me and asked me if I would join him outside. We made out. A lot. I had made plans to spend the night at my friend's. He said he would like to stay with me, and I certainly had no problem with that, and I asked my friends who said they had no problem with it. Then, Zayne begged me to come back to his place. I said no the first eight times, but then I caved (RED FLAG #1). I was drunk and he was very cute when he was begging and I kind of loved that he wanted to be with me that badly.

Since we had both been drinking, Zayne's friend drove us back to his apartment. I was mad during the car ride though, because, despite all of the begging, Zayne sat in the front seat with his friend (RED FLAG #2). That felt rude to me, so I took another gulp of vodka and swallowed about my feelings. Then, I remembered he had a snake, so before actually going to his place, I asked about it and he assured me it was at his dad's house. Within minutes, we were in his room. He apologized for his room being messy, and it was really, really messy. I don't even remember there being sheets on his mattress (RED FLAG #3) … despite all of these signals, I continued to make out with him. Then we slept together. I don't really remember sleeping together though… parts of it but it definitely happened. After it was over, he went to the bathroom, and I was so drunk and sleepy that within seconds I fell asleep.

This is where it gets painful for me to talk to you about… but if you have gotten this far with me, you deserve to know.

It felt like it had been hours later when I woke up. I was in a dark room that I had never seen before. No one was in the room with me. My stomach ached so badly and I could hardly move. I realized I was naked. I was cold. I was scared. I tried to find my clothes in the dark but I couldn't so I picked a t-shirt up off of the ground and pulled it on to cover me. I thought I was going to be sick. I walked out of the room I was in, to see Zayne, sleeping on the couch with his bros around him.

I remember feeling so little in that moment and wondering why he wasn't sleeping next to me.

I thought he might have a reason for not sleeping next to me, though. I hoped for a second chance. I hoped that if I woke him up, he would take care of me (he had promised he would at the party).

I woke Zayne up. I told him I wasn't feeling well. He found some Tylenol, gave it to me, and then I went back to try to fall asleep…

I heard Zayne came back into his room and I got nervous and excited. He laid down next to me and suddenly the atmosphere felt like -200 degrees. There was no affection, no kindness.

It was Antarctica in that room.

I faked being asleep. Within minutes, he went back out to the living room. What did I do wrong? I laid in that bed for an hour silently crying (as not to wake any of the guys in the other room) with tears rolling down my face, so embarrassed, so lonely, so dark, so quiet.

I decided I couldn't take it any longer. It was six a.m., with shaking hands, I got my phone out and called Tiff, hoping that she might answer despite the time. She did. She answered on the second ring. She asked me where I was, I told her I didn't know and then she told me to send her my location. I sat on the floor, trying to gather up everything that I knew was mine.

Then I spotted that awful bottle of Grey Goose Vodka. It was expensive, but the look of it made me sick, so I left it behind. Within fifteen minutes, Tiff came and picked me up.

When I opened Zayne's bedroom door, I wondered if I should tell him goodbye, or say anything, but I had nothing to say. I walked past where he was sleeping, and I couldn't even bring myself to look at him. Something felt wrong, and lonely, and dirty.

When I got in Tiff's car, she didn't pry, which I appreciated. She was there for me. She dropped me off at my apartment and as soon as I shut the door behind me, I began to cry. I cried so hard I threw up. I couldn't look at my reflection. I felt wrong, lonely, dirty, used.

Our story doesn't end there, though. After that night we didn't really talk a lot. Then two months after it happened, it was still sitting with me wrong. I decided to text him for answers. He was so honest with me. He told me that he had real feelings for me and that he was afraid of getting hurt again. I understood that completely. He was out of town for the weekend, but he asked for another chance to take me out and date me when he got home - a Monday date. Nothing bad ever happens on a Monday date, right? I agreed to it. Sunday night, I texted him about the details of our Monday date. His response was, "What are you talking about?", and I reminded him of the plans we had made. He said, "Sorry, I was super drunk all day and don't remember making those plans. I'm not interested in dating anyone right now". I was livid. A fit of anger, livid. He was texting me completely coherent sentences about being with me. I know drunk texting and that was not it.

I tried to make sense out of the situation for days, weeks, months following until I finally understood everything. He didn't care about me. He got what he wanted out of our interactions and it was just sex. A body. It could have been any body, but mine was available to him that night.

If you're out there actually reading this, man or woman, know your self-worth...

Know that you are valuable…

Know that you are worthy of affection…

Know that there is more out there than being only a sexual object to someone.

Zayne and I didn't work out. Despite everything I went through, I still search for some sort of approval from him. A part of me still hopes I will get an explanation from him one day. Maybe he was in a bad place, too. Maybe he was in love with me and it scared him… Maybe he was in love with someone else, and he needed company so bad he was willing to sacrifice my feelings to get it. I don't know. I love to dream, to hope, to believe in the best of people. The weirdest part is, I genuinely think he is a good person, he just did some bad things.

With our interests matching up, the way I always felt pulled to him from the very first moment I met him in school, every level we connected on, what we wanted to do with our lives after college - all of it made me feel like we were supposed to be together. His energy was something that mine matched up with really well. It all made sense on paper to me so I started believing in love, again. I thought he was going to be that crazy story I would have about meeting him when I was younger, and us falling in love, and la la la dee da. Mistake. Mistake. You should never give someone else that much power over your happiness. Ever. Lesson learned.

I got my hopes up. He dropped them on the ground and stomped on my hopes without remorse. Maybe without even realizing he had… I hope he becomes more responsible as he gets older with other people's emotions. After everything, I still think he is a cool person, just a bit reckless.

With love always,

Delilah

<u>Zayne's Playlist</u>

Brooklyn – Fickle Friends

Heart of Glass – Blondie

Cheerleader – St. Vincent

Infinity – The XX

Sex – The 1975

Breathe Me – Sia

Crown of Love – Arcade Fire

Perfect Illusion – Lady Gaga

Beast of Burden – The Rolling Stones

Venus Interlude

Every side of me is torn, yet I know I am still a
masterpiece. How many of the great arts are in
perfect condition? Venus De Milo is missing her arms
and yet, she is iconic. I will be too. Iconic that
is. Not a statue without arms.

With love, always,

Delilah

Anonymous's Chapter

Hello Confidant,

    I did mention this at the beginning but I do fall in love with people so easily. I wasn't really looking for love when I ran into this person, which meant that love was going to find me. It found me this time, on a busy summer morning at a restaurant where I worked. We had a huge breakfast rush and after hours of buzzing around, I finally had a break to get myself and the sticky countertop clean. As I was scrubbing away at the counter, I began singing a song in my head. I got lost in the lyrics, "I never sat by the shore..." I glanced up and noticed someone had been waiting for me to re-enter this world. He was smiling a patient smile. I was stunned by his presence as I had not even noticed that he walked up. He was gorgeous. Very dapper looking, in fact. I apologized for not noticing him sooner and he politely told me it was fine", that he wasn't in a hurry. I took his order and while he was waiting around, we began to talk.

    In our conversation, I discovered he was a medical student, studying to be a heart doctor, and I thought to myself "how ironic because he is making my heartthrob".

He was smart and handsome and polite and he thanked me for helping him as if it wasn't my job to do so and after a while of the conversation, he left. I wish I could say there was more after that, but there wasn't, ever. For days after he stuck around in my head. Our encounter felt so intense and right that I thought I had my fairytale moment where he was going to be my one true love.

Then, practical sense reminded me that I was a young adult that had discovered the feeling of "lust". I was charmed by his manors, good looks, and success, but I knew nothing about his personality deep down. At that moment, being able to come to that conclusion I realized that I was growing up. I took responsibility for my pettiness, for jumping the gun.

With the right person, if that fairytale moment does really ever happen, it's not going to be about whether they're good looking or have a successful career. It will feel right. Or at least, I hope it does but I won't stop being ready to embrace it. I want love, I know I deserve it, and I have so much to give.

With love always,

Delilah

The Remedy

The air outside feels warm, cozy, familiar. I feel the disillusion of happiness creep over me as the sunshine spills in through my windows. How do you feel now? I feel like tackling the world today. Putting it all out there, being vulnerable… it really is terrifying. I challenge you to try it. Don't be quiet about what is upsetting you. You have one life to live. Are you really going to let other people live it for you? I'm not anymore. I've learned that the people who are meant to be in your life will be. Anyone who you have to walk on eggshells to make happy isn't worth your time.

There is no manual for navigating life. Sometimes when the bad stuff happened to me, I couldn't help but wonder "do I deserve this?", "is it something I did wrong?". Questioning yourself like that will eat you up as quick as a witch named Betty.

I'm so young and I still have so much to learn but I want to help other people, too… so I will share my experiences, my aches, my remedies - here, of course: a comfort zone, a safety net. A computer screen where the other person on the other end is unknown. How exciting, how thrilling, how romantic. I am writing for no one and everyone all at once. For me. For you, confidant. Whoever you are. I'm thankful for you. A part of me loves you already. Please don't betray that trust. If you do, I know how to handle it now… but it would be best for us if you didn't.

Some of this stuff was really hard to endure. I won't lie to you now. I had some really, really bad days, but I survived with blind optimism. There is no way to be able to tell if something is going to get better. Just keep being a good person. As cliché as it is, continue to treat other people the way you want to be treated. Maybe romantic love won't fall right into your lap right away, but friendship might. A better relationship with your family might. You have to keep being optimistic.
From everything that happened to me, I grew, I learned confidence. confidant.

And when you deal with all of that pain, and you're trying to navigate such tough water, you have to remember your oars. And if your oars let you down, you'll probably have a life vest, or a buoy, or a green light. There will be something to keep afloat, something to hold on to, something to keep reaching for. I promise. It'll be there. You have to see it, reach out, and grab it.

So here is my remedy or guide to get through:

-Be a nice human

-Decide you want to be happy and then *be* happy. Do something every day to work towards inner happiness.

-Don't let your past hold you back; it's the past, it's behind you. Leave it there.

-Put yourself first sometimes, and don't feel bad about it.

-Surround yourself with love. You are so worthy of it, and you have so much to give, confidant. Thank you for staying with me through all of this. Until next time!

With love, *always*,

Delilah.

Made in the USA
Columbia, SC
08 February 2019